AF584802

For Carmen, Emma, Katrina and Suzanne—D.F.
For Heath. You bring so much colour into our lives.—J.H.

Scholastic Australia
An imprint of Scholastic Australia Pty Limited
PO Box 579 Gosford NSW 2250
ABN 11 000 614 577
www.scholastic.com.au

Part of the Scholastic Group
Sydney • Auckland • New York • Toronto • London • Mexico City
New Delhi • Hong Kong • Buenos Aires • Puerto Rico

Published by Scholastic Australia in 2023.

A catalogue record for this book is available from the National Library of Australia

ISBN: 9781761291968

Typeset in Argone LC and Flapstick

Printed in China by RR Donnelley.

Scholastic Australia's policy, in association with RR Donnelley, is to use papers that are renewable and made efficiently with wood from responsibly managed sources, so as to minimise its environmental footprint.

10 9 8 7 6 5 4 3 2 24 25 26 27 / 2

How to START SCHOOL in 6 Easy STEPS

DHANA FOX

JAMES HART

A Scholastic Australia Book

Rosie was starting school.

Apparently, starting school was easy.
It said so in Rosie's new book.

Rosie got her **uniform** ready for school.

BUS
STOP

The next morning, Rosie packed her lunchbox and raced to the bus stop.

Rosie was ready to start her first day at school.

Step One:
Don't Be Late.

'Has the bell gone? What did I miss?'
'Let us out!'

Step Two:
Find Your Classroom.
'Er . . . can I follow you?'
'I'm being hunted!
Help!'

Step Three:
Meet Your Teacher.
'My name's Rosie.
I lost fifteen teeth in the holidays.'
'That's . . . lovely,
Rosie.'

Step Four:
Set Up Your Desk.

CRACK
'Take cover!'

Step Five:
Get to Know
Your Classmates.
'Mmm, you smell like the sea.
Do you want to be my lunch buddy?'
'Lunch? I'm not your lunch!'

There was one final step.

Rosie was so excited.

Step Six:
Be a Brave Learner.

'Pick me! Pick me!'

'My name's **Rosie**.
I'm **five and a quarter** years old.
I love extra-large **seals**.
My eyes can **glow** in the dark.
And my favourite **colour** is . . .'

'Rainbow!'

Where did everyone go?
Rosie wondered.

No-one wanted to hear
All About Rosie.

Her first day at school wasn't
going well at all.

Until . . .

'Rosie looks sad.'
'Maybe she isn't scary after all.'
'Let's cheer Rosie up.'

'I know what we can do!'

'We made this for you, **Rosie!**'
'I'm **five and a quarter** years old too!'
'My bottom can **glow** in the dark!'
'And here's your very own **desk.**'
ROSIE

Rosie couldn't believe it.

The entire class was smiling . . .
at her?

Amazing!

'Thanks, everyone! This is the best rainbow ever!
Chase you to the bus stop!'

Rosie couldn't wait for school to start the next day. And the next. And the next . . .

SCHOOL